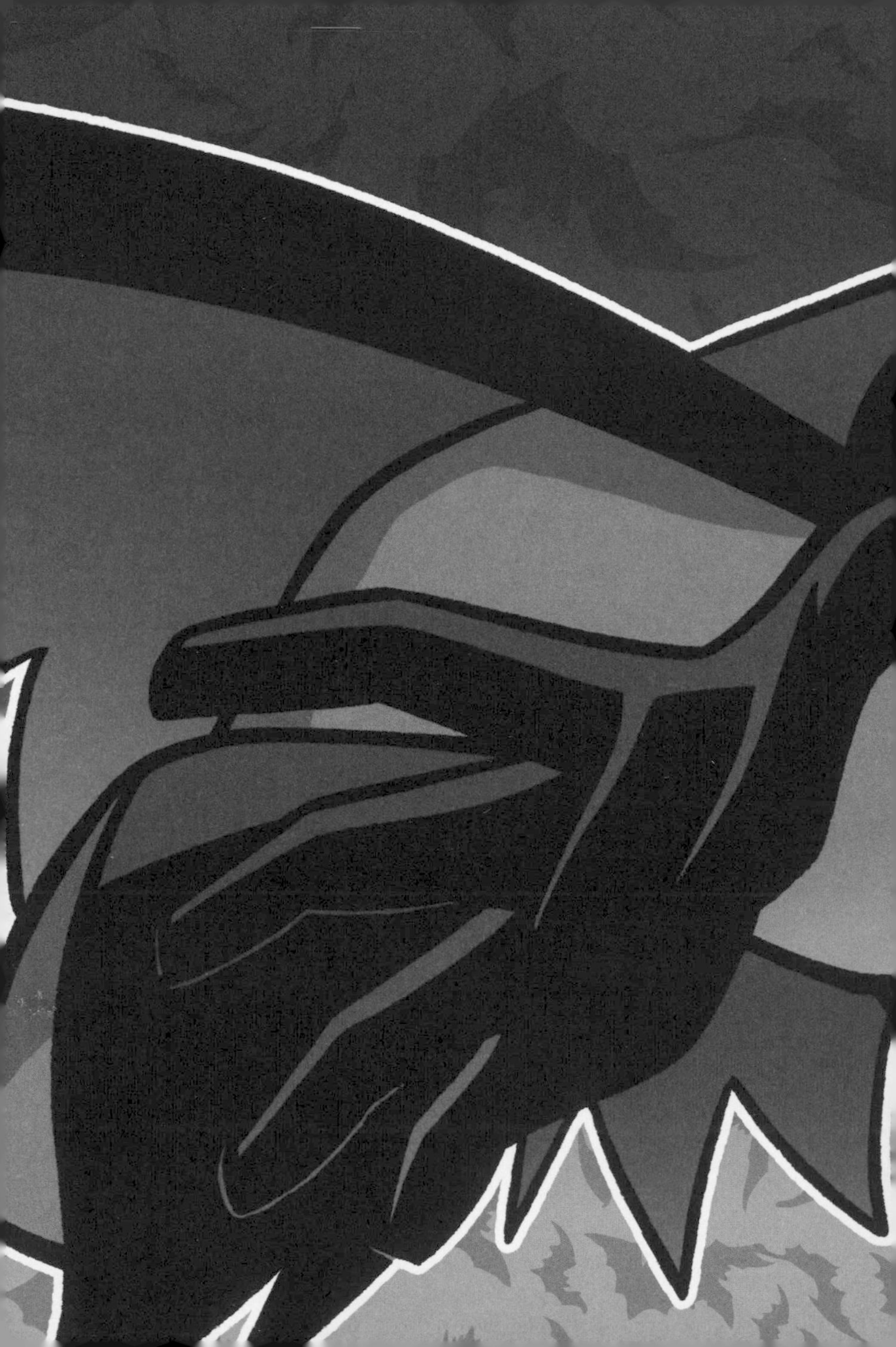

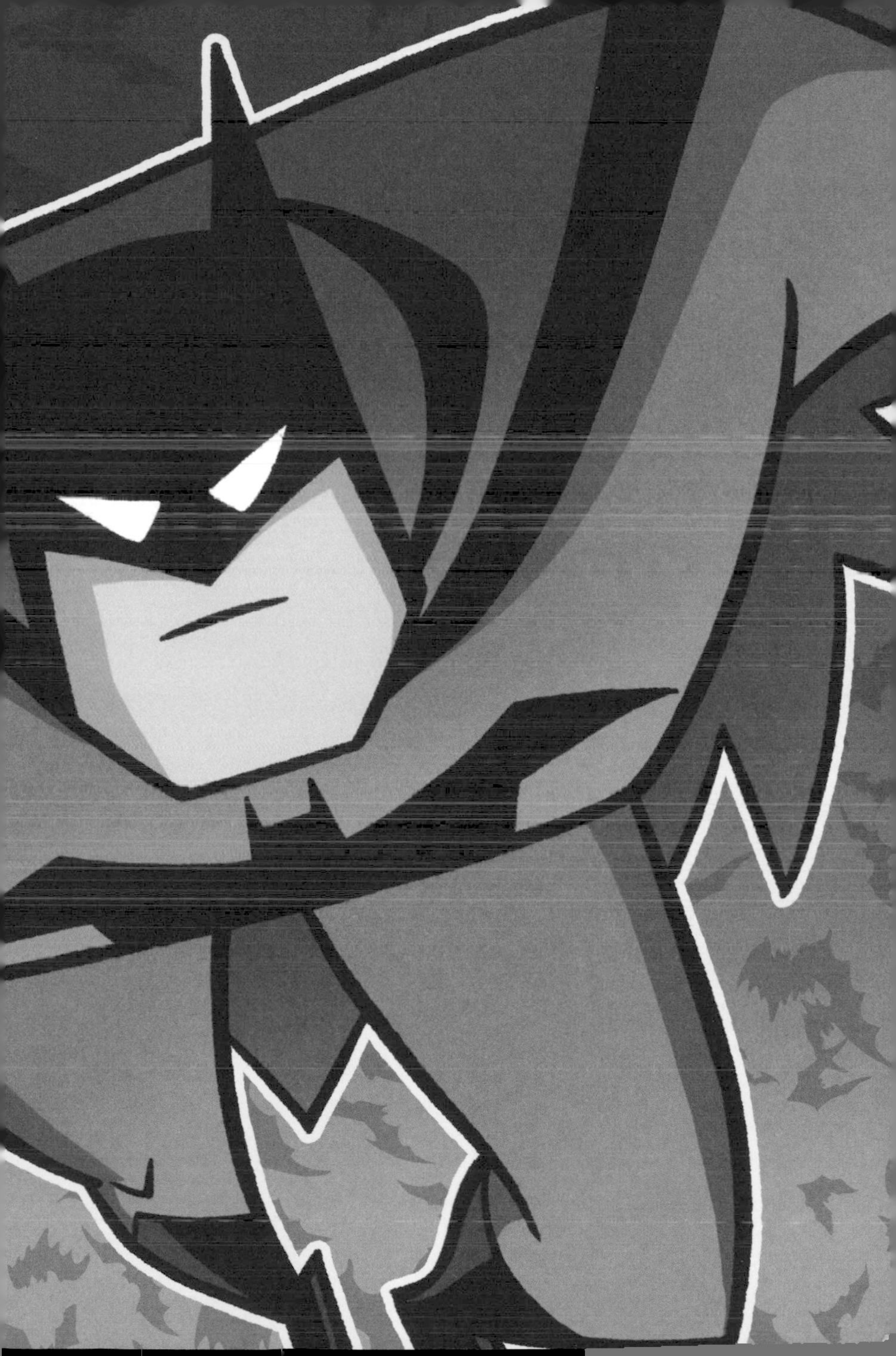

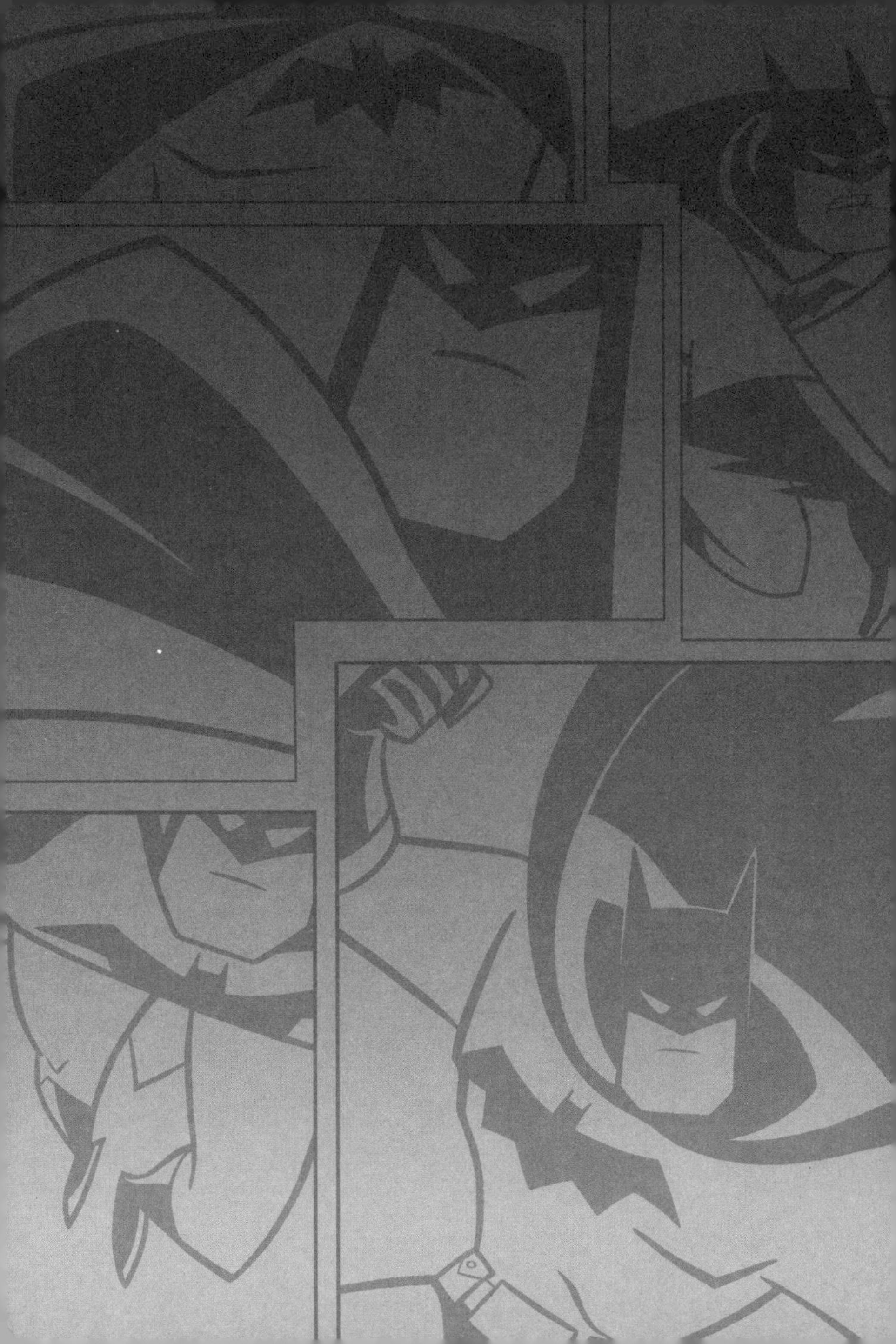

DC COMICS SUPER HEROES

BATMAN

MAD HATTER'S MOVIE MADNESS

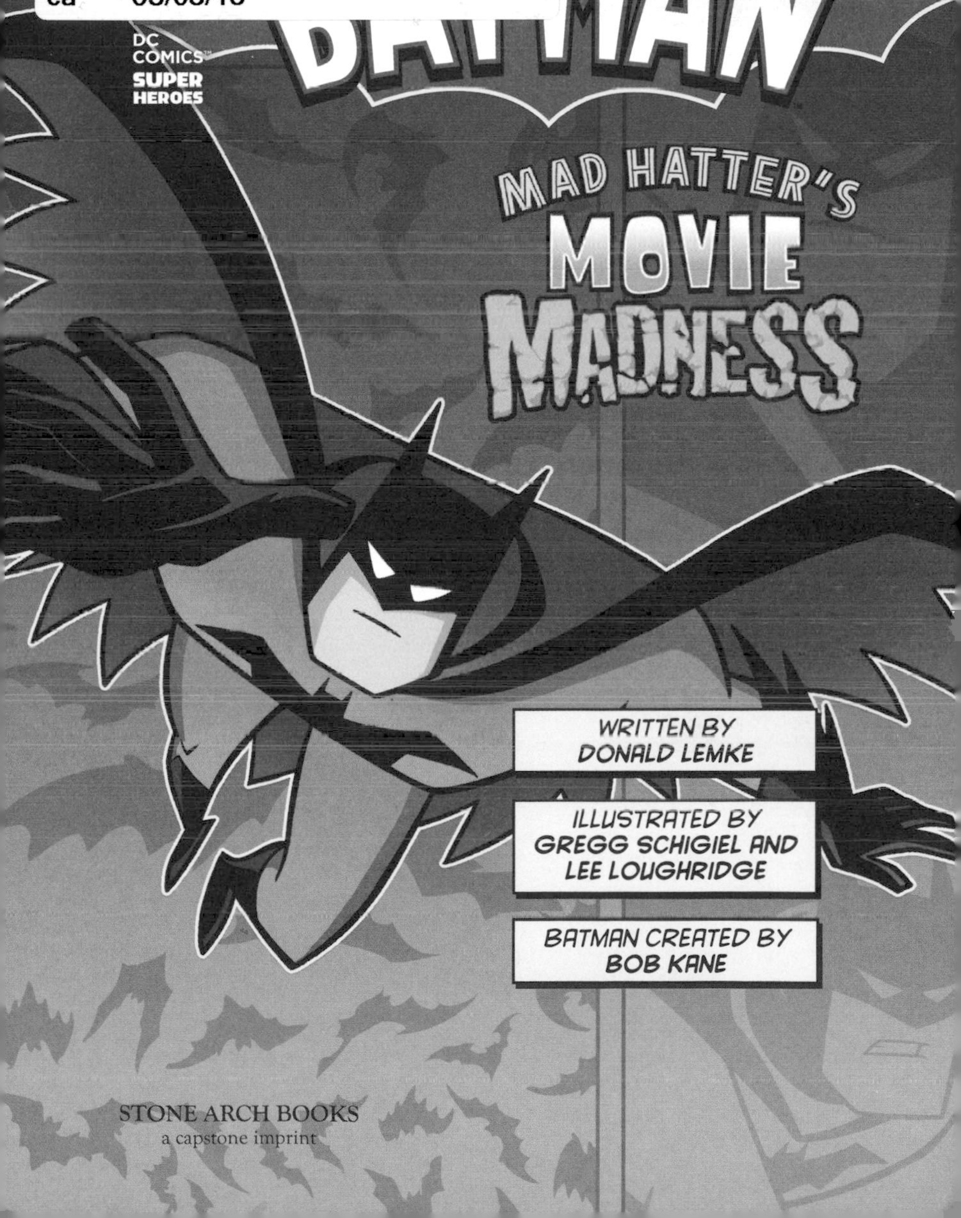

WRITTEN BY DONALD LEMKE

ILLUSTRATED BY GREGG SCHIGIEL AND LEE LOUGHRIDGE

BATMAN CREATED BY BOB KANE

STONE ARCH BOOKS
a capstone imprint

Published by Stone Arch Books
A Capstone Imprint
1710 Roe Crest Drive
North Mankato, Minnesota 56003
www.capstonepub.com

STAR13132

Cataloging-in-Publication Data is available at the Library of Congress website.

ISBN: 978-1-4342-2131-5 (library binding)
ISBN: 978-1-4342-1675-5 (paperback)

Summary: Billionaire Bruce Wayne and his teenage sidekick, Tim Drake, have
tickets to a new Alice in Wonderland movie. Unfortunately, Jervis Tetch, also
known as the Mad Hatter, has infiltrated the theater and installed his micro-
circuitry into the 3-D glasses. When the movie begins, dozens of Gotham teens
are brainwashed! That night, Tim and the other teens awake, rush to the Mad
Hatter's lair, and receive instructions to rob the city's jewelry stores. They obey
the demands, but soon run into Batman! The Dark Knight must follow the
teens, stop the Mad Hatter, and save the Boy Wonder from Wonderland.

Art Director: Bob Lentz
Designer: Brann Garvey
Production Specialist: Michelle Biedscheid

Printed in the United States of America in Stevens Point, Wisconsin.
052013   007387R

TABLE OF CONTENTS

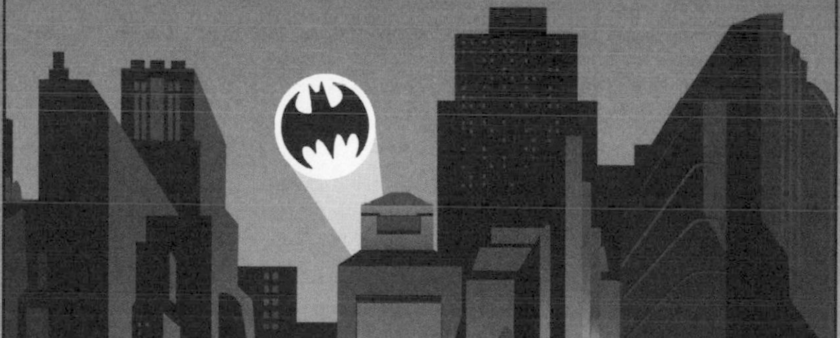

CHAPTER 1

BIG SCREEN BRAINWASH

Tim Drake stepped out of a limousine in front of the Gotham City Cinema. Reporters lined the red carpet. **CLICK! CLICK!** They snapped photos of the city's most elite citizens. Through the blinding camera flashes, the teen looked up at the theater's marquee. The title of the movie, *The New Adventures of Alice in Wonderland 3-D*, glowed in big, bright letters on the sign.

"What's wrong?" asked Bruce Wayne, following Tim out of the limo and giving him a shove. "Not used to the attention?"

"Ha!" Tim laughed. As the secret super heroes Batman and Robin, Bruce and Tim had faced far greater challenges than the paparazzi. "I just can't believe you scored tickets to the year's biggest premiere!"

"My company owns the theater," replied the billionaire with a wink. "Now, come on. We're going to miss the previews."

Bruce and Tim hurried past the crowd and headed inside. Except for a few people buying last-minute candy and popcorn, the cinema's lobby was nearly empty.

"I knew we should've gotten here earlier," said Tim, starting to worry. "All of the good seats are probably taken!" He grabbed Bruce by the elbow and pulled him toward the ticket booth. A theater worker waiting behind the counter grinned widely as they approached.

"Are we late?" Tim asked the usher.

For a moment, the worker stood in silence, adjusting the small hat atop his head and continuing to smile. Then he reached into the pocket of his uniform and pulled out a giant watch.

"What a funny watch!" Tim exclaimed. "The hands are running backward!"

The usher's grin quickly disappeared. "I've seen feet run, but never hands," the man said with a serious face. "Perhaps you are the funny one."

"No, you didn't understand," said Tim, trying to explain. "I meant that the time on your watch is counting down."

"Yes, but half the time it's counting *up*," the usher replied, holding the watch toward Bruce and Tim.

The man pointed at the second hand, which was spinning counter-clockwise. "See! On one side the hand goes down, and on the other side the hand goes up. I'd say it's counting around and around."

"Huh?" Tim asked. "No, I meant —"

"We're here for the premiere," Bruce interrupted, shoving the tickets toward the strange man.

"Certainly," the usher replied. He took the tickets, slowly tore them both in half and then returned the stubs. "But, of course, the show has already started."

"Why didn't you say so?!" Tim exclaimed. He grabbed Bruce again and dashed toward the main theater.

"Wait!" shouted the theater worker as they left. "You forgot your 3-D glasses!"

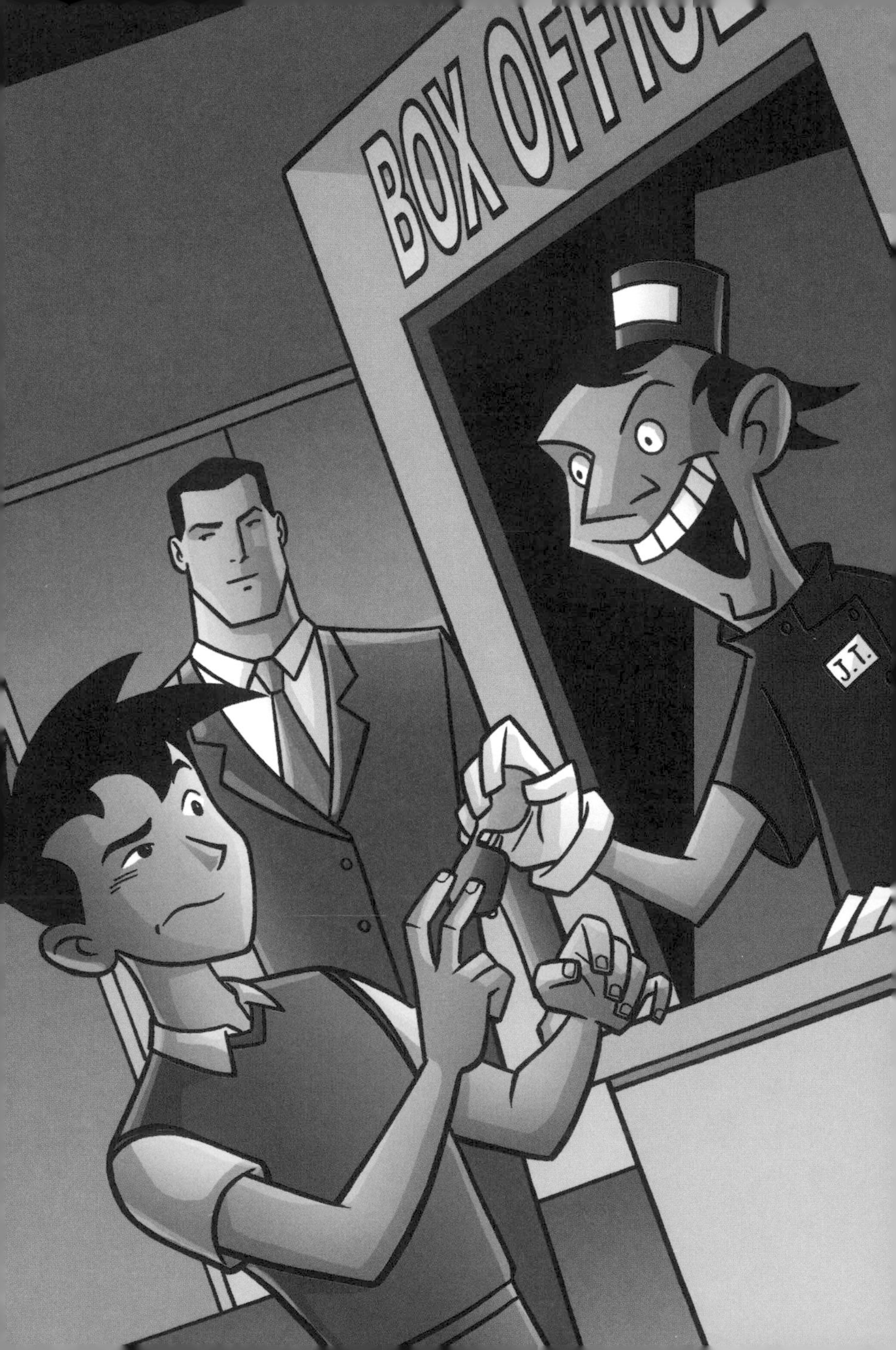
BOX OFFICE
J.T.

Tim turned and stormed back toward the man behind the counter. Gritting his teeth, the frustrated teenager held out his hand. "Thank you," he grumbled.

"You wouldn't want to forget these," said the worker, handing Tim two pairs of plastic glasses. "I heard the special effects are mind blowing!" *HAHAHAHA!*

As the usher's laugh echoed through the empty lobby, Bruce and Tim headed into the darkened theater. The previews had already started, and the audience stared up at the glowing movie screen. Each person wore a pair of the special 3-D glasses.

"There!" Tim whispered to Bruce, pointing toward two empty seats in the middle of the second row. The teenager ran down the aisle and quickly took his seat.

Bruce followed closely behind. "Excuse me. Pardon me," said the billionaire, attempting to squeeze through the same crowded row. "If I could just —"

 Bruce glanced down at the sticky theater floor. A pair of 3-D glasses had been crushed beneath his shoe. Suddenly, a little girl began to cry.

"Hey! Those were my daughter's glasses!" said an angry woman sitting next to the child.

"Sorry, ma'am," apologized Bruce. "Here! Take mine, little girl." He handed the child his own pair of 3-D glasses. She quickly stopped crying.

"But you'll miss the special effects," whispered Tim from his seat.

"Don't worry," said Bruce. "I'll get another pair." He turned and headed back up the aisle.

In the lobby, Bruce stood at the ticket booth and waited for the strange usher to return. But after few a moments, he decided to ask someone else for help.

"Excuse me," said Bruce, approaching the concession stand. "Do you know where the man with the 3-D glasses went?"

"Yeah, that dude flaked," replied the annoyed teen behind the counter. "He said something about 'time' being up and then quit. The guy only worked here one day!"

"Are there any extra glasses?" asked Bruce.

"They're probably next to his old uniform," said the teen.

The teen pointed at a crumpled pile of clothes near the ticket booth. "Feel free to check," he said. "I have to get back to work."

Bruce quickly searched the area near the uniform. He lifted the usher's coat, gave it a shake, and set it back down. Then he noticed a silver nametag attached to the chest, etched with the initials "J.T."

For a moment, Bruce wondered what the initials stood for. Then a roar of laughter erupted from inside the main theater.

"The movie must have started!" Bruce said to himself.

He gave the area one last look and then rushed back inside the theater — without a pair of 3-D glasses.

CHAPTER 2

A MAD TEA PARTY

Later that evening, as a thunderstorm gathered in the darkened sky, Bruce and Tim returned to Wayne Manor. Bruce Wayne's loyal butler, Alfred Pennyworth, greeted them at the mansion's front door.

"So how was the movie, Master Tim?" asked Alfred, taking the teen's jacket and shaking off a few drops of rain.

Tim shrugged his shoulders. "Eh," he said, eyeing Bruce. "It was . . . all right."

"Oh, come on," said Bruce.

The billionaire removed his coat and handed it to Alfred as well. "You're not going to hurt my feelings," he said. "Tell him what you really thought of the movie."

"It was awesome!" Tim exclaimed. "Possibly the best movie of the year! Maybe even the greatest 3-D movie of all time! And the special effects . . . unbelievable."

"Okay, okay," said Bruce. "Now can we go to bed?"

"What's the matter, Master Bruce?" asked the butler.

Tim leaned in toward Alfred. "He broke some kid's 3-D glasses and had to give her his pair," explained the teen.

"I chose to give her my glasses, Tim," Bruce interrupted. "And, by the way, you can probably take yours off now."

"No way," said Tim, adjusting his own 3-D glasses. "These are a collector's item. I can't wait to show them off at school." The teen sprinted up the spiral staircase toward the second floor of the mansion. "Thanks again for the tickets, Bruce," he shouted down from his bedroom doorway.

Bruce stood at the bottom of the stairs, shaking his head. "Can you believe that, Alfred?" he said. "A grown boy attached to some cheap plastic glasses. Who would want such a silly souvenir?"

"Shall I search for another pair online, sir?" asked Alfred.

"You know me too well," said Bruce. He gave the loyal butler a pat on the back and headed up the stairs. "Goodnight, Alfred."

"Goodnight, sir." he replied.

That night, as most of the city slept, a heavy rain pounded downtown Gotham. Far beneath the flooded streets, a man wearing a top hat and a bow tie paced back and forth inside a room filled with high-tech machinery. He reached into his purple overcoat, pulled out an oversized pocket watch, and smiled.

"Tick tock," said the man, laughing. "It's almost time for the time I have planned!"

He scurried around the room, flipping switches and pulling levers on a giant control panel. Then he sat in front of a microphone and placed his hand over a glowing, red button. As his pocket watch started to chime, the man pressed down.

CLICK! "Wake up!" he screamed into the microphone. "The Mad Tea Party is about to begin!"

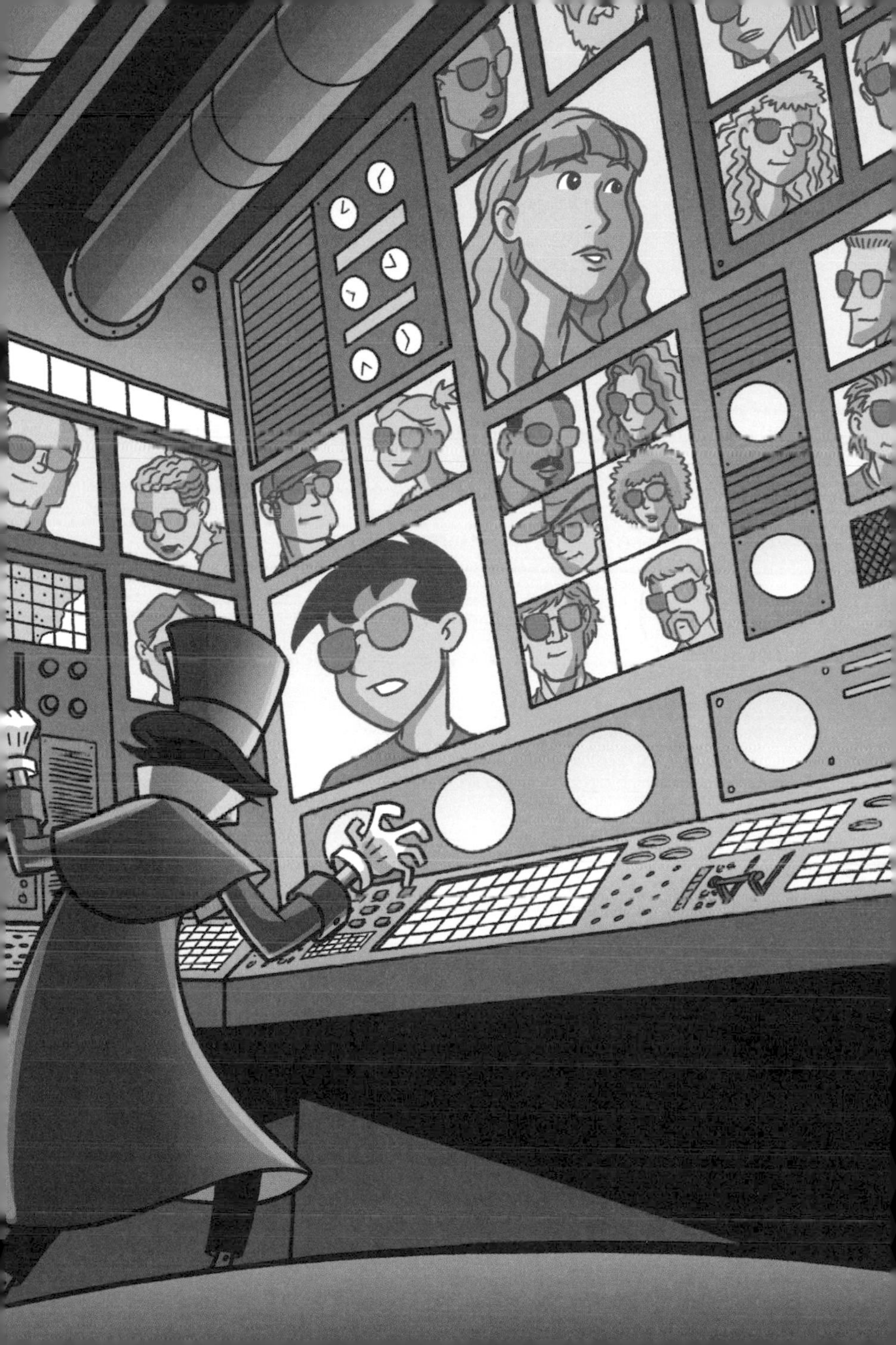

Meanwhile, back at Wayne Manor, an explosion of thunder rattled Tim's bedroom windows. The digital alarm clock on his nightstand flickered 11:59 PM in glowing, red numbers. Tim had dozed off nearly an hour ago, reading his favorite comic book and still wearing his clothes and 3-D glasses. The storm hadn't awakened the teen, but then the clock struck midnight.

Tim's eyes opened wide, and he sprang up in bed. "I'm late! I'm late!" shouted the teen. **SPROING!** He bounced onto the floor like a jackrabbit and rushed out of the bedroom. "I shall be too late!"

Tim sprinted down the staircase and opened a passageway on the first floor. At the bottom of another flight of stairs, he entered the Batcave, a secret storage facility for the Dynamic Duo's equipment.

In a panic, Tim hopped onto a Batcycle, revved the motorbike's engine, and sped out of the cave toward Gotham City.

Within minutes, he arrived downtown, skidding to a stop at the corner of Dodgson Avenue and Main Street. Tim quickly jumped off the Batcycle and waded through the ankle-deep puddles until he heard a hollow sound beneath his shoes. He kneeled down and lifted off a manhole cover. *SPLASH!* A flood of dirty, brown water poured into the opening.

"I'm late! I'm late!" Tim repeated. Then he leaped into the deep, dark hole and landed in a shallow canal of sewer water below. A maze of underground tunnels stretched out in every direction. But even in the dark, Tim somehow knew exactly which way to go.

Within moments, he spotted light coming from a small doorway at the end of a tunnel. Tim crept toward the tiny entrance, bent down, and peeked inside.

"Come in! Come in! There's plenty of room!" shouted a gap-toothed man in a large top hat. He was standing at the head of a long dinner table, speaking into an oversized microphone. Dozens of guests surrounded the table, sipping tea from giant cups.

Tim slowly entered the room, which was filled with buzzing machinery. As he sat down in the last open chair, the other guests turned their heads and stared at him with dazed eyes. Each person wore a pair of identical 3-D glasses.

"Every good crime begins with tea," said the man into the microphone.

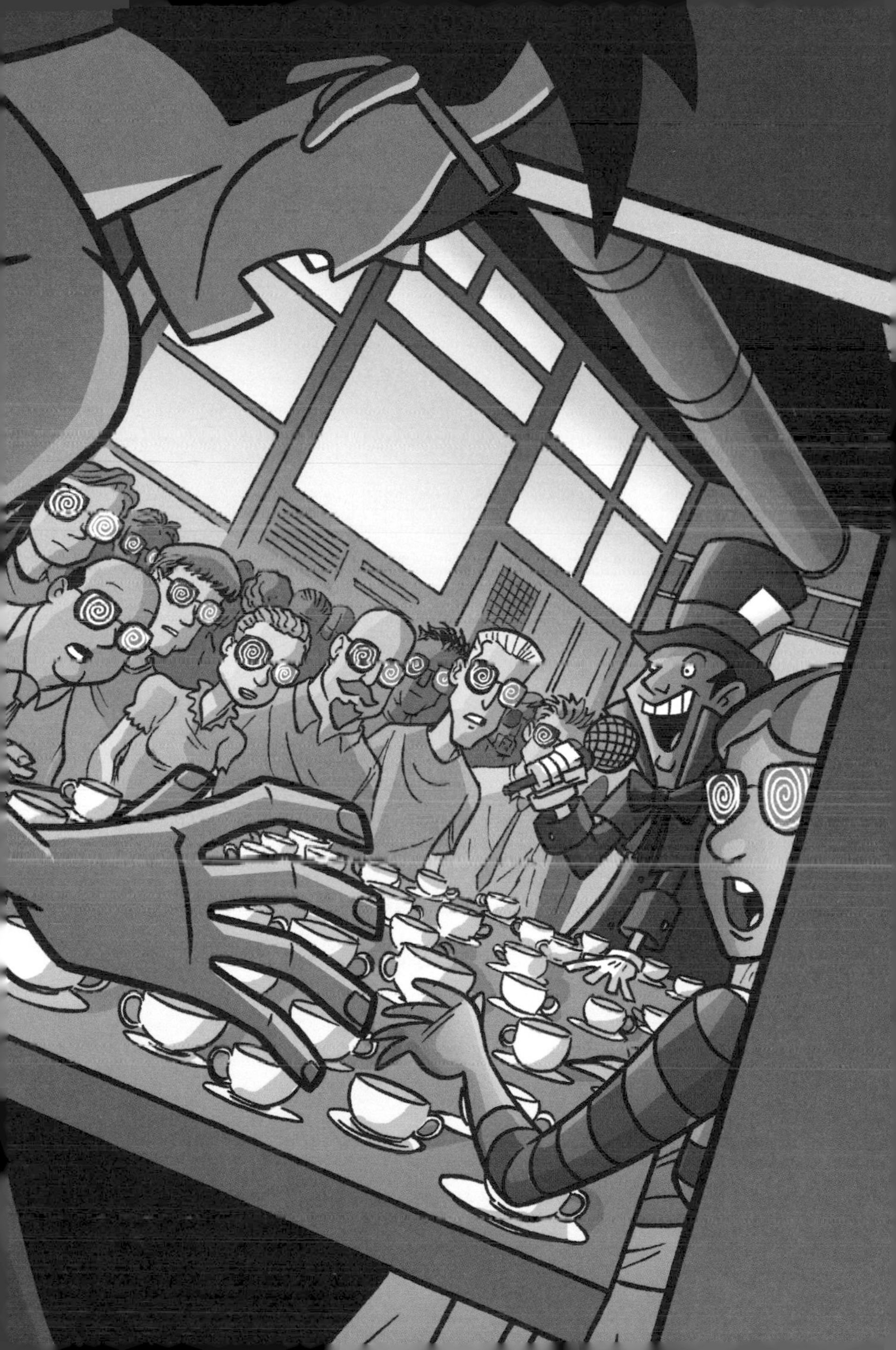

The obedient guests turned their attention back to their host. "Well, 'crime' actually begins with C, doesn't it now?" he continued. "But, of course, I didn't bring you here to spell 'crime.' My spell brought you here to commit one."

With his microphone, the strange man walked toward a control panel and switched on a video monitor. KLIKKK! An image of an attractive blonde woman suddenly appeared on the screen.

"To win the heart of my lovely Alice," shouted the madman, pointing toward the video screen, "it'll take a roomful of diamonds. And you will get them for me!"

Tim and the other guests stood up from the table, and together they replied, "Yes, master."

CHAPTER 3

BOY WONDER IN WONDERLAND

Later at Wayne Manor, an alarm sounded in Bruce's bedroom. The billionaire awoke, threw on a robe, and calmly walked down the upstairs hallway. As Batman, an alarm at three o'clock in the morning would never startle the secret super hero. But when he arrived at Tim's bedroom, something did surprise him.

Tim was gone.

Bruce hurried down the spiral staircase and met Alfred on the first floor. "Have you seen Tim?" he asked the butler.

"I assumed he was behind you, sir," Alfred replied. "You know how he likes to sleep in."

"Not today," said Bruce, rushing through the secret passageway to the Batcave.

As Bruce quickly changed into his Batsuit, Alfred checked the Batcomputer for information about the alarm. "Several jewelry stores in Gotham have been robbed, sir," said the butler. He turned and looked toward the Batcycle's empty parking spot. "And, it appears Master Tim is already on the case."

Bruce approached the Batmobile and slid inside the driver's seat. He switched on the vehicle's computer. The dashboard lit up with hundreds of buttons and several radar monitors. One screen displayed a map of downtown Gotham City.

Dozens of glowing, red lights on the screen showed the locations of each jewelry theft. A single yellow light blinked on and off near one of the markers.

"That's the Batcycle," said Batman, pointing at the yellow light. "You're right, Alfred. Tim must have gotten a head start."

"Perhaps this is his way of paying you back for the movie tickets," the butler said.

Batman hit a switch to open the cave's secret exit. "Doesn't he know, Alfred," said the Dark Knight with a smile, "I do this stuff for free." Then he fired the Batmobile's ignition and raced into the night.

Following his radar screen, Batman arrived a short time later at the corner of Dodgson and Main. He stepped out of the Batmobile and spotted the Batcycle.

As the Dark Knight approached the abandoned machine, he nearly fell into the open manhole Tim had uncovered a few hours earlier.

Batman kneeled near the opening. Heavy rainwater continued to flood into the sewer below, washing away any clues, such as footprints or tool marks.

Splash! Splash! Over his shoulder, the Dark Knight heard a gang of teenagers dashing through the streets. "We're late! We're late!" they yelled. "This way!"

Batman spun around and squinted through the pouring rain. The teenagers were running toward him, away from Don's Jewelry Store on the other side of the street. Each of them carried a large, black bag, and each wore a strange mask with a different animal face.

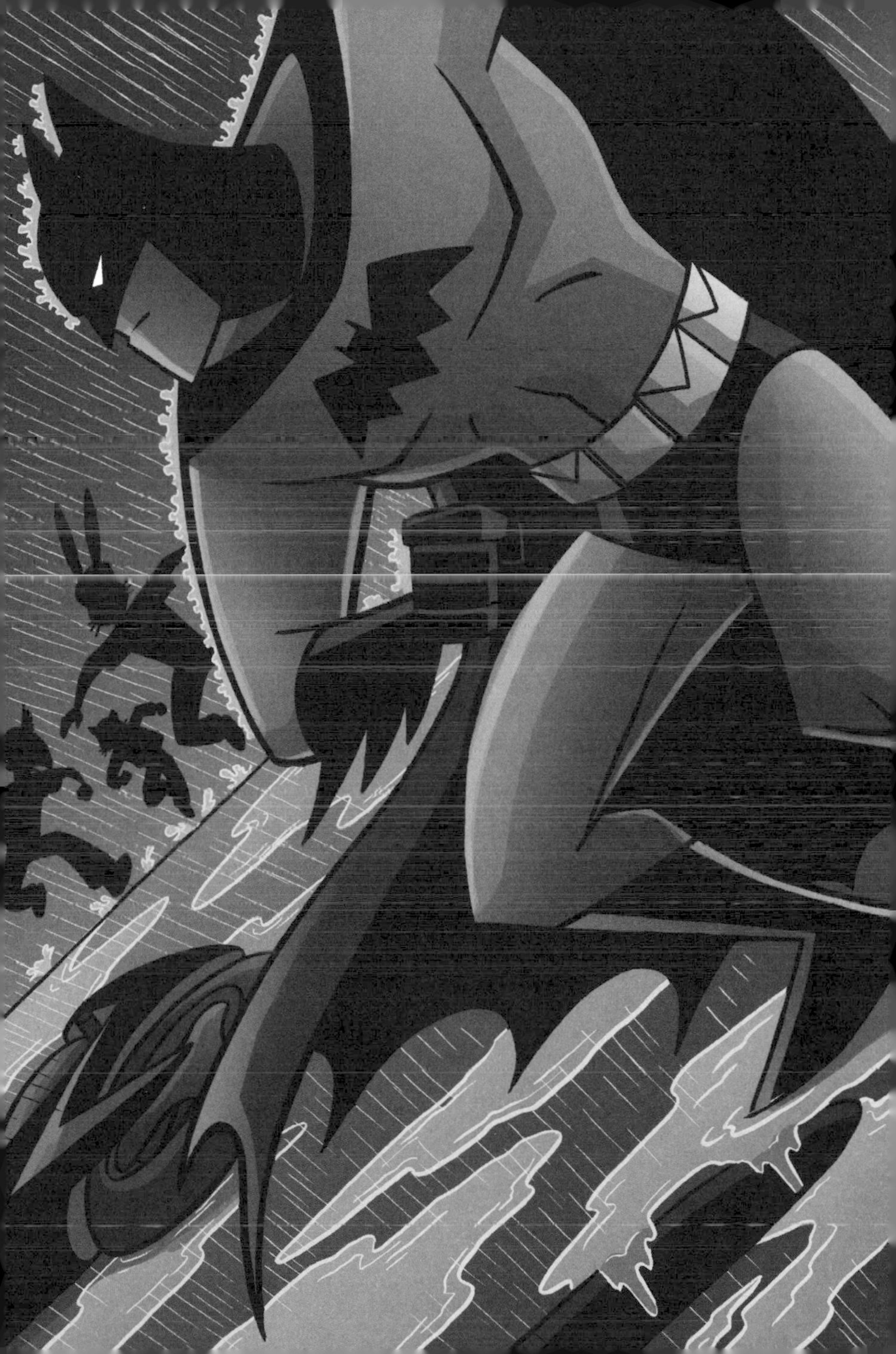

The Dark Knight leaped into the air. A second later, he landed next to the teenager wearing the mask of a grinning cat. "Not so fast," said Batman, snagging the crook by the collar. He grabbed the teen's black bag and looked inside. It was filled with diamonds and other valuable jewels. "Just as I thought."

Batman pushed the cat-faced crook aside and searched for the other thieves. He spotted another thief, wearing the mask of a white rabbit, about to escape down the manhole. Without hesitating, the Dark Knight reached into his Utility Belt, pulled out a Batarang, and threw it toward the thief. **FWIP! FWIP!** A super-strong wire unraveled behind the weapon and wrapped around the thief's ankles. **THUD!** The crook fell face-first onto the flooded street.

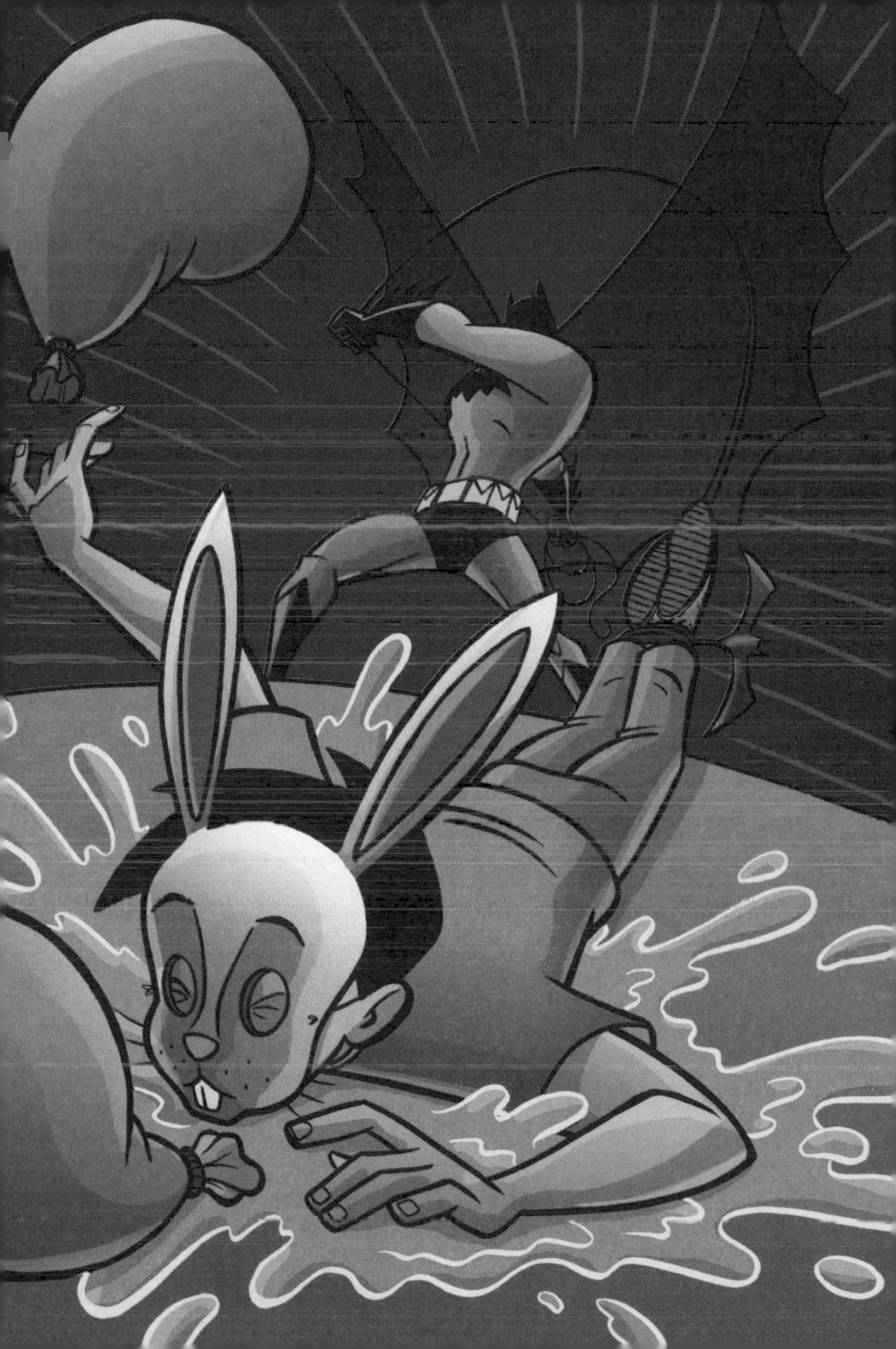

Batman walked to the fallen criminal. He crouched on the wet asphalt and flipped the crook onto his back. "Let's see who you really are," said the Dark Knight. He grabbed the rabbit mask and pulled it off.

"Tim?!" exclaimed Batman.

The teenager stood and looked around in a daze. Behind him, the other masked crooks were jumping into the open manhole, escaping through the sewers.

Before Batman could react, Tim grabbed the mask from the ground. He ripped off one of the rabbit ears and placed the mask back on his face. Then he turned and leaped into the manhole.

A moment later, the Dark Knight went down after him, never once considering the danger he was getting into.

CHAPTER 4

DOWN THE RABBIT HOLE

Down, down, down, Batman fell through the manhole and splashed into the sewer below. When he looked up in the tunnel, Tim and the other crooks were gone.

The Dark Knight stared at his hand. He was still holding the torn piece of mask. "A rabbit ear," Batman said himself. "What was Tim trying to tell me?"

The World's Greatest Detective rubbed the piece between his fingers. Right away, he knew the mask had been made from several layers of heavy-duty cardboard.

Between the layers, Batman felt a pattern of thin ridges, like the veins of a leaf. He pulled at the rain-soaked edges of the cardboard, slowly separating each layer. In the middle, Batman found a web of wires connected to a tiny microchip.

"I should have known," said the Dark Knight, recognizing the technology. He thought about the faces of the masks again. A grinning cat. A dormouse. A white rabbit. Characters from the book *Alice's Adventures in Wonderland.* "This can be the work of only one man." **CRUNCH!** Batman crushed the sparking microchip in his wet glove. "The Mad Hatter," he growled.

Batman had faced the villain many times before. He knew the Mad Hatter used this type of device to brainwash innocent victims into committing crimes.

"How could he have brainwashed Tim?" the Dark Knight asked himself. "I was with him the whole night at the movies."

Then Batman recalled the strange usher at the theater. His gap-toothed smile and puzzling riddles suddenly made sense. "Of course!" shouted the Dark Knight. He remembered the initials "J.T." etched on the usher's nametag. Now Batman knew that the letters stood for "Jervis Tetch," the true identity of the of the Mad Hatter.

"Jervis must have installed his brainwashing microchips into the 3-D glasses," concluded Batman. "I guess the special effects really *were* mind blowing."

Then suddenly, the Dark Knight heard a loud rumbling coming from behind him. The ground beneath his feet began to shake.

Batman spun around, expecting to see a subway train barreling down the tunnel. Instead, he saw a wall of storm water crashing toward him. **WHOOOOSH!**

The wave knocked Batman off his feet. Within a moment, he was up to his chin in dirty water, swirling through the sewers. He tried to stop himself by digging his gloves into the wall. Sparks flew from his fingertips, but the rushing water pulled him deeper into the tunnels.

Barely able to breathe, Batman reached into his Utility Belt. He pulled out his grapnel gun, aimed at a sewer pipe above him, and fired. **CLANK!** The metal grapnel hook latched onto the pipe. The Dark Knight quickly pushed the Recoil button on the gun, and a super-strong wire pulled him safely out of the water.

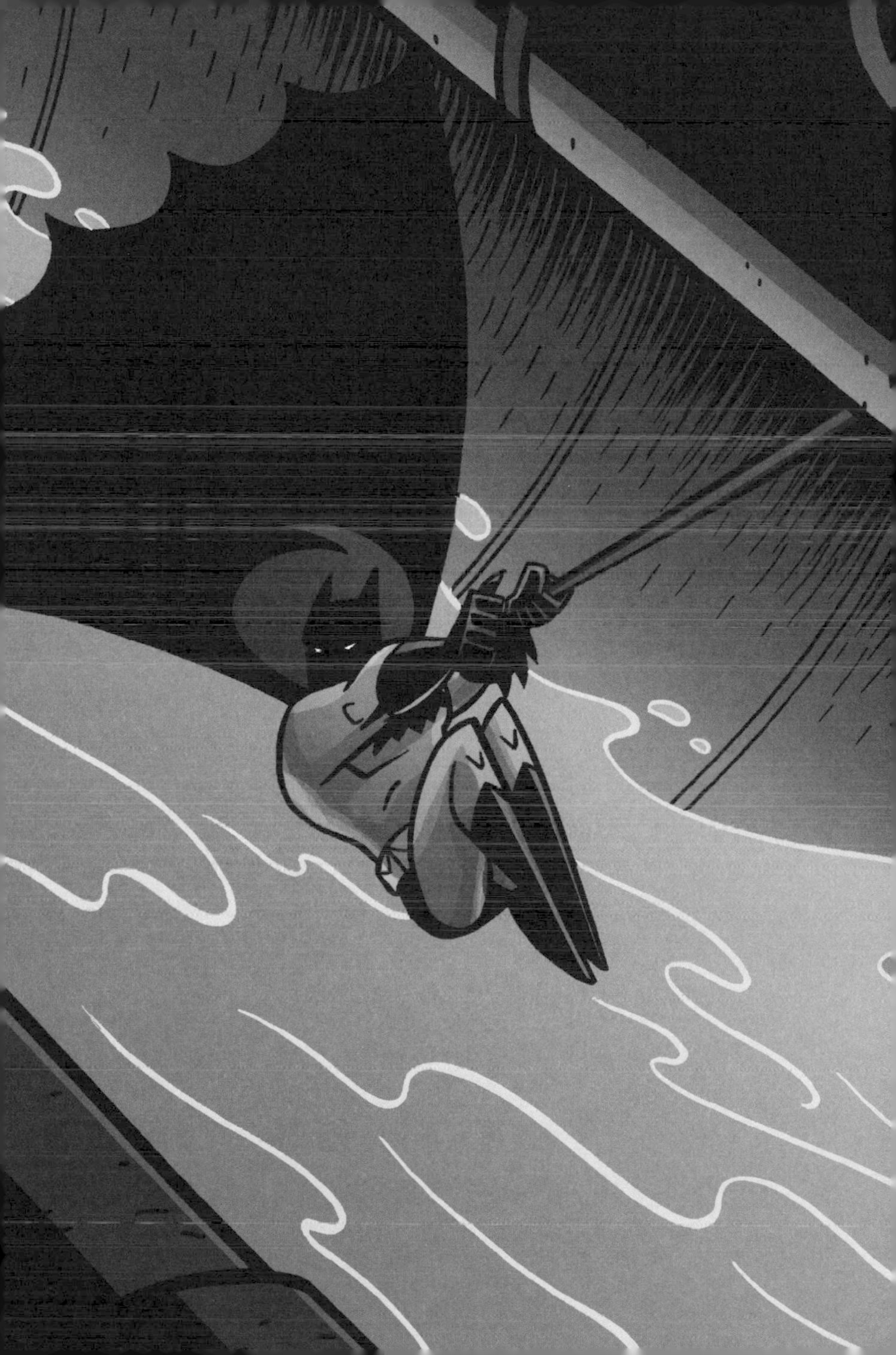

Dangling from the ceiling, Batman suddenly spotted one of the masked criminals. He was sitting on a nearby sewer pipe, wearing the mask of a grinning Cheshire cat.

"Where's the Mad Hatter?" shouted the Dark Knight.

The cat-faced crook pointed farther down the tunnels. "In that direction," said the masked thief, "lives a Hatter."

"Which way?" asked Batman, frustrated by the situation. The super hero knew he couldn't harm the brainwashed teen, but he needed more information.

"That depends on which way you want to go," the teen replied.

"It doesn't matter which way," added Batman. "As long as I get there."

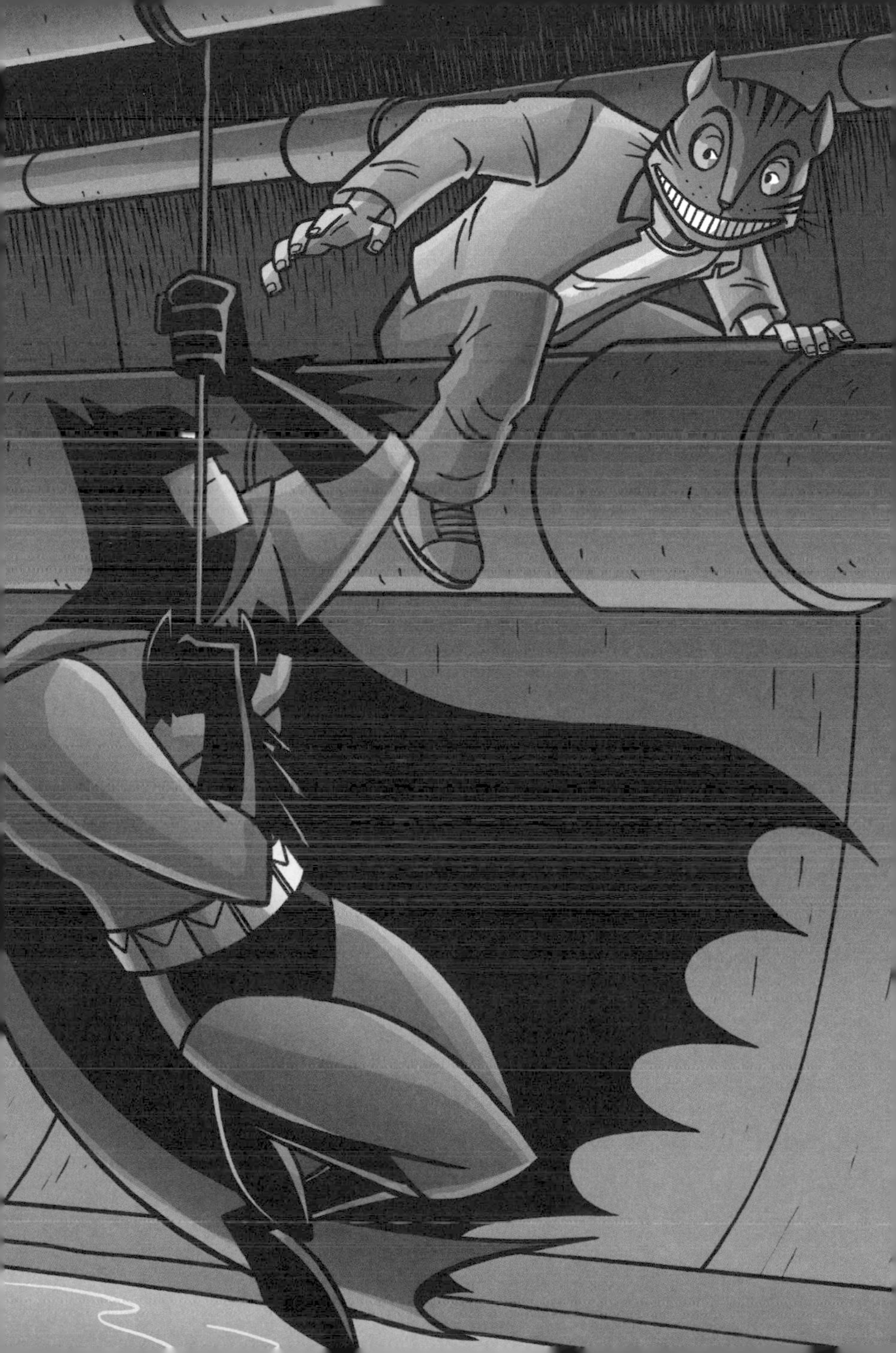

"Oh, you're sure to do that," said the cat-faced crook with a laugh, "if you only walk long enough." The brainwashed teen jumped from the pipe and splashed into the canal below.

By now, the rushing water had passed, and the sewer was shallow enough to wade through once again. Batman quickly released his grapnel gun. He landed in the canal and took off behind the cat-faced crook, following his splashes through the pitch-black tunnel.

A short time later, the noises stopped. The boy had somehow disappeared.

Batman continued slowly down the tunnel until he reached a dead end. "Where did he go?" the Dark Knight asked himself. He felt the stone wall in front of him, searching for a secret passage.

Then near his feet, he spotted the top of a tiny doorway, nearly hidden in the dirty, brown water. Batman kneeled and opened the entrance. As water spilled into the opening, the Dark Knight held his breath and crawled inside.

On the other side of the door, Batman stood and listened. The room was silent and dark. But then, before he could turn on his night-vision lenses, the lights suddenly came on. **CLICK!**

Batman was surround by dozens of brainwashed people, each wearing a different paper mask. And, in the middle of them all, stood their leader, the Mad Hatter.

"Welcome," shouted the crazy criminal, "to my Mad Tea Party!"

CHAPTER 5

OFF WITH THEIR HEADS!

"Thanks for the invite, Hatter, but I have other plans!" replied Batman. He lunged toward the crazed super-villain.

"Get him!" shouted the Mad Hatter into his microphone.

The brainwashed crowd obeyed their master. A dormouse, a Cheshire cat, and other masked characters leaped at Batman and quickly tackled him to the ground. The Dark Knight tried to get up, throwing people left and right. **POW! SLAM!** Soon, however, he stopped.

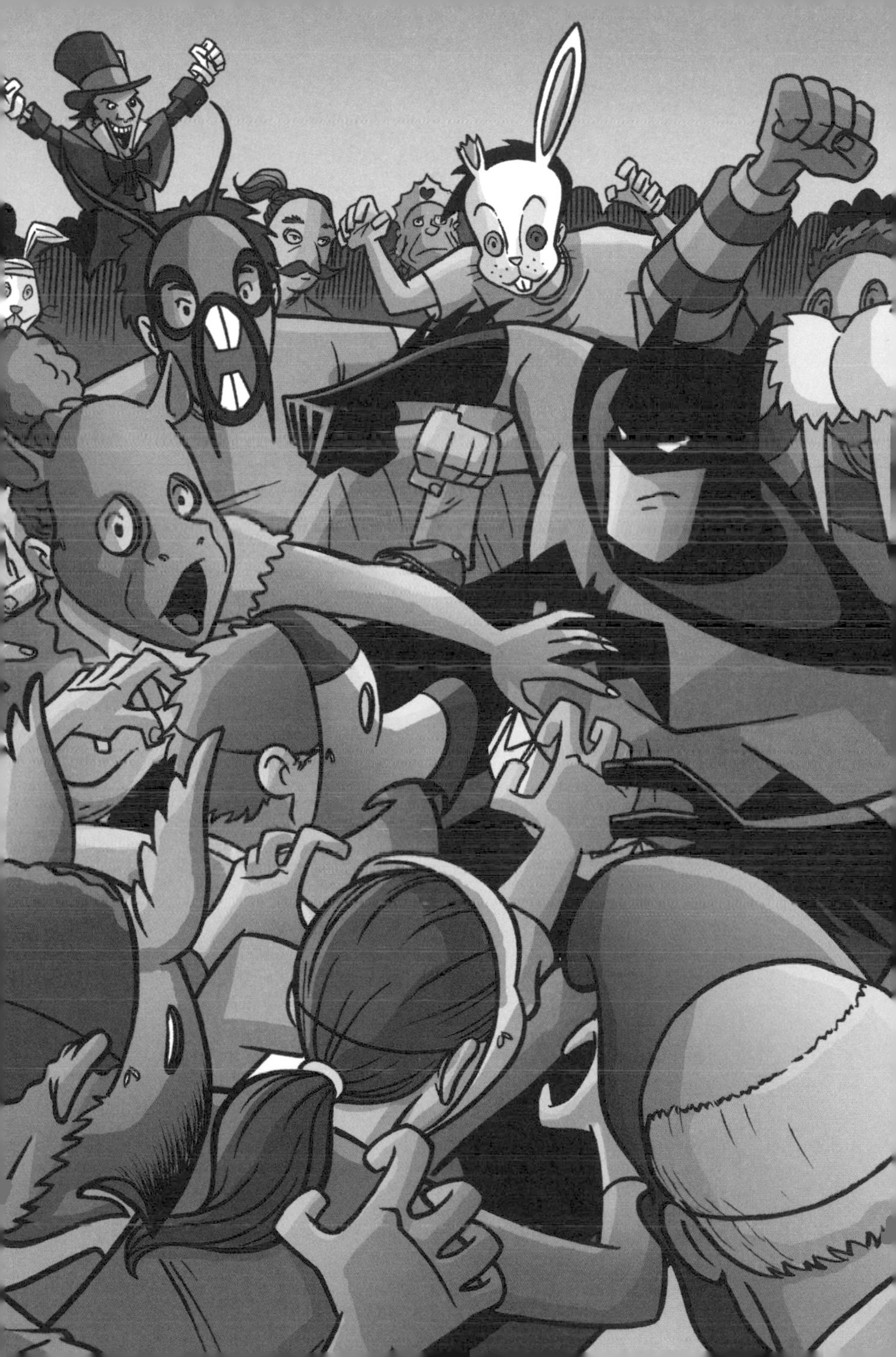

These are innocent people, thought Batman. *I have to capture the Mad Hatter without hurting them.*

The Mad Hatter looked amused by his foe's lack of effort. "What's the matter?" he said. "Giving up so soon?"

"You'll never get away with this, Hatter," said Batman.

"Oh, really?" replied the crazy crook. The Mad Hatter waved his hand, and the obedient crowd parted. Behind them, a large garbage dumpster was completely filled with diamonds and jewels. "It appears I already have, Batman."

The Mad Hatter walked to the dumpster and dug out a fistful of gems. "You see," continued the villain, "with these diamonds, I'll win back my beloved Alice."

"And then," he continued, "we'll rule all of Gotham. The King and Queen of Hearts!"

While the Mad Hatter spouted his crazy plan, Batman scanned the room. He searched for a way out of the situation, but time was quickly ticking away.

Suddenly, the Batman spotted something that made him smile. Through the crowd, he saw a single rabbit ear poking above the other masks. *Tim*, he thought.

Batman quickly turned his attention back to the Mad Hatter. "That's a great plan, Hatter, but there's one, little problem," said the super hero. "Alice will never take you back."

"And why not?" shouted the villain.

"Because you're mad!" replied Batman.

"Don't you think I know that?" squealed the Mad Hatter. He spread his arms and looked around the room. "I'm mad. You're mad. We're all mad here!" HAHAHAHA!

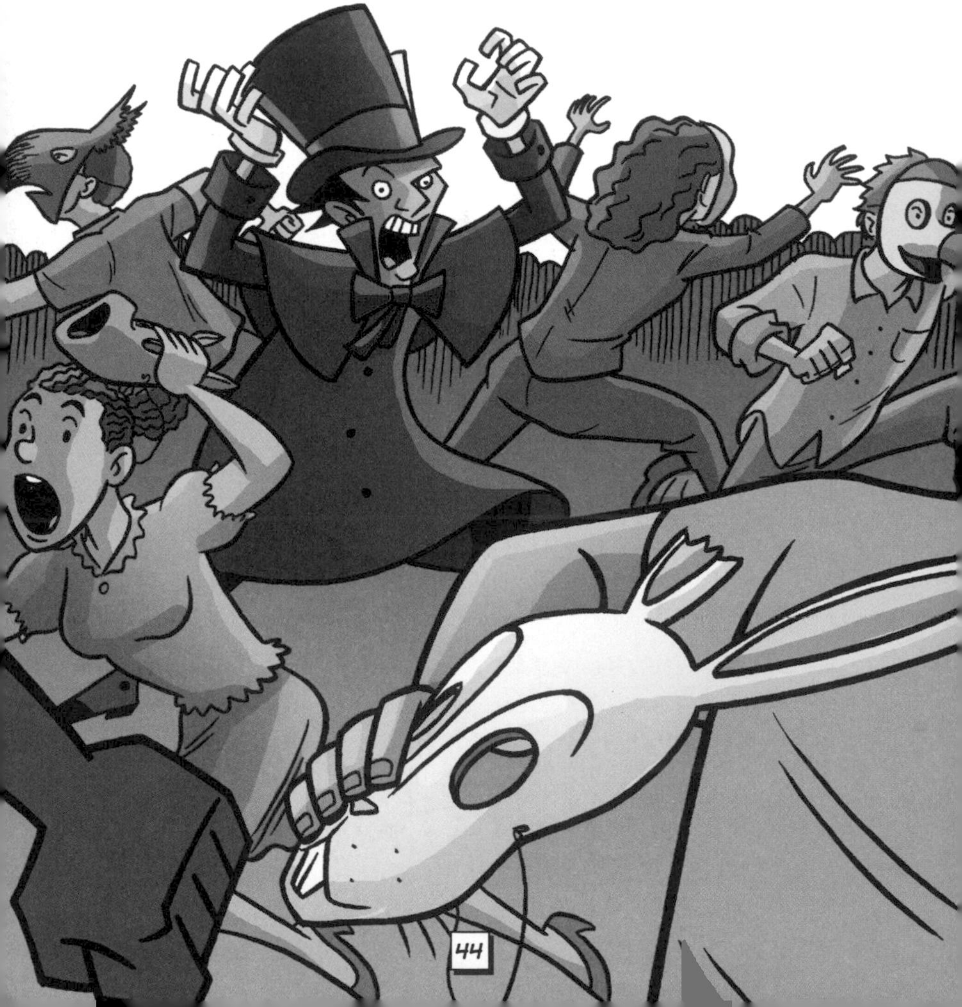

Just then, Tim jumped from behind the crowd and pulled off his mask. "Speak for yourself!" he shouted. "Now, Batman — off with their heads!"

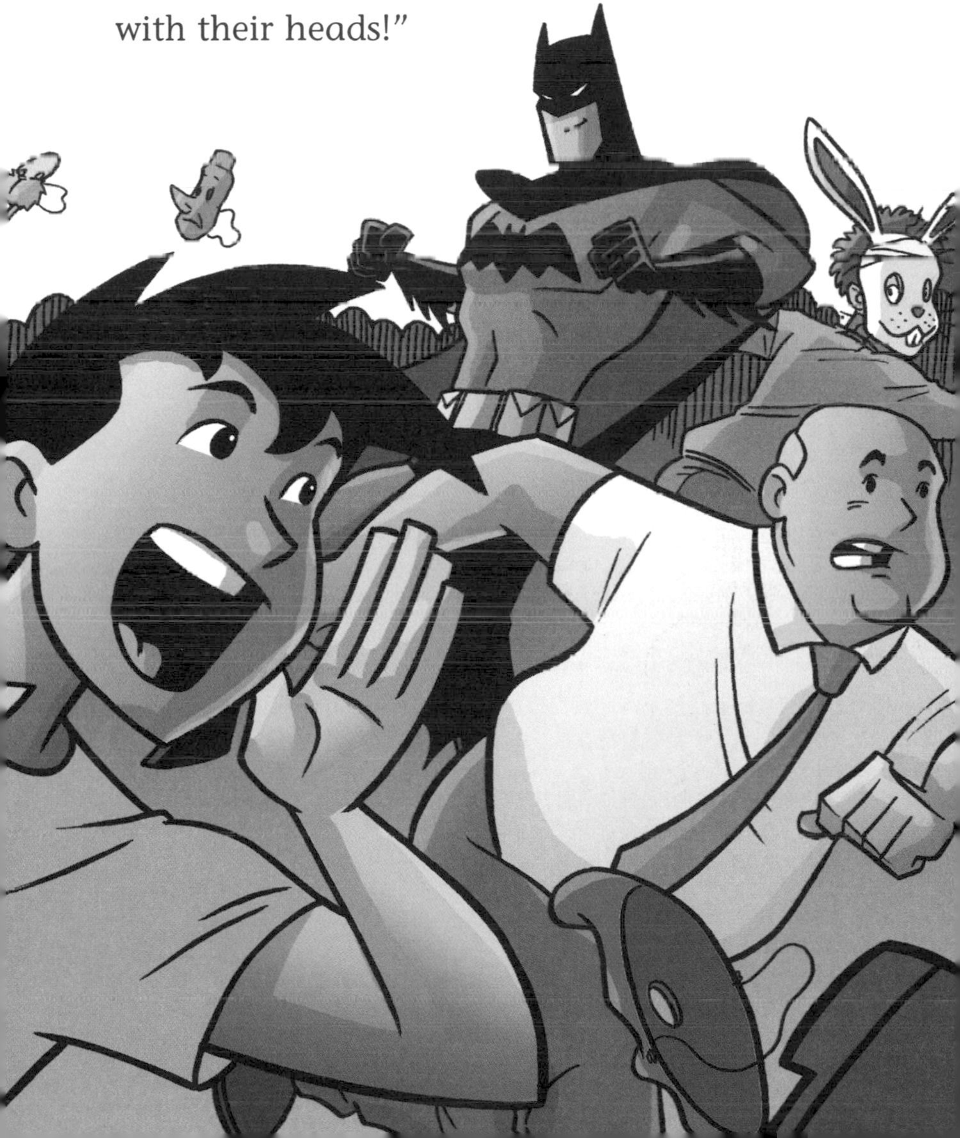

The Dark Knight followed his partner's lead. The Dynamic Duo circled the room, snatching the paper faces off each of the brainwashed victims. Within seconds, the tables had turned, and the Mad Hatter was now the one outnumbered.

"Nooooo!" the villain screamed. He threw his microphone onto the floor and made a break for the exit.

No longer under his spell, the mob surrounded the crook. The crowd had remembered everything that happened while they were brainwashed. They weren't about to let the villain get away.

A few minutes later, Batman led the crowd through the sewers to the open manhole. The rain had stopped, and the Gotham City Police had arrived to help people back onto the street.

Once everyone else was safe, Batman climbed up the hole with his prisoner. He handed the Mad Hatter to several officers. "Let him watch the sunrise," Batman said, pointing toward the horizon. "It might be the last one he sees for a while."

The Dark Knight turned and walked over to his teenage sidekick. "Okay, Tim," started Batman. "I think I figured out what happened. Hatter installed his devices into the 3-D glasses, brainwashing everyone at the theater — except me, of course. Then he installed the same microchips in the masks, which is why you robbed the diamond store."

Tim nodded.

"But, when I pulled off your mask here on the street," Batman continued, "the spell was broken, right?"

Tim nodded again.

"Then I only have one question for you," asked the Dark Knight. "Why didn't you tell me you were no longer brainwashed?"

"I didn't want the Mad Hatter to know his plan had been foiled," Tim replied. "At least not until you reached his hideout."

"Good thinking," said Batman. "Patience is a sign of a mature hero."

"And," Tim added with a smile. "You never got to see the 3-D *Alice in Wonderland* movie. I figured, this way you'd get to star in your own version!"

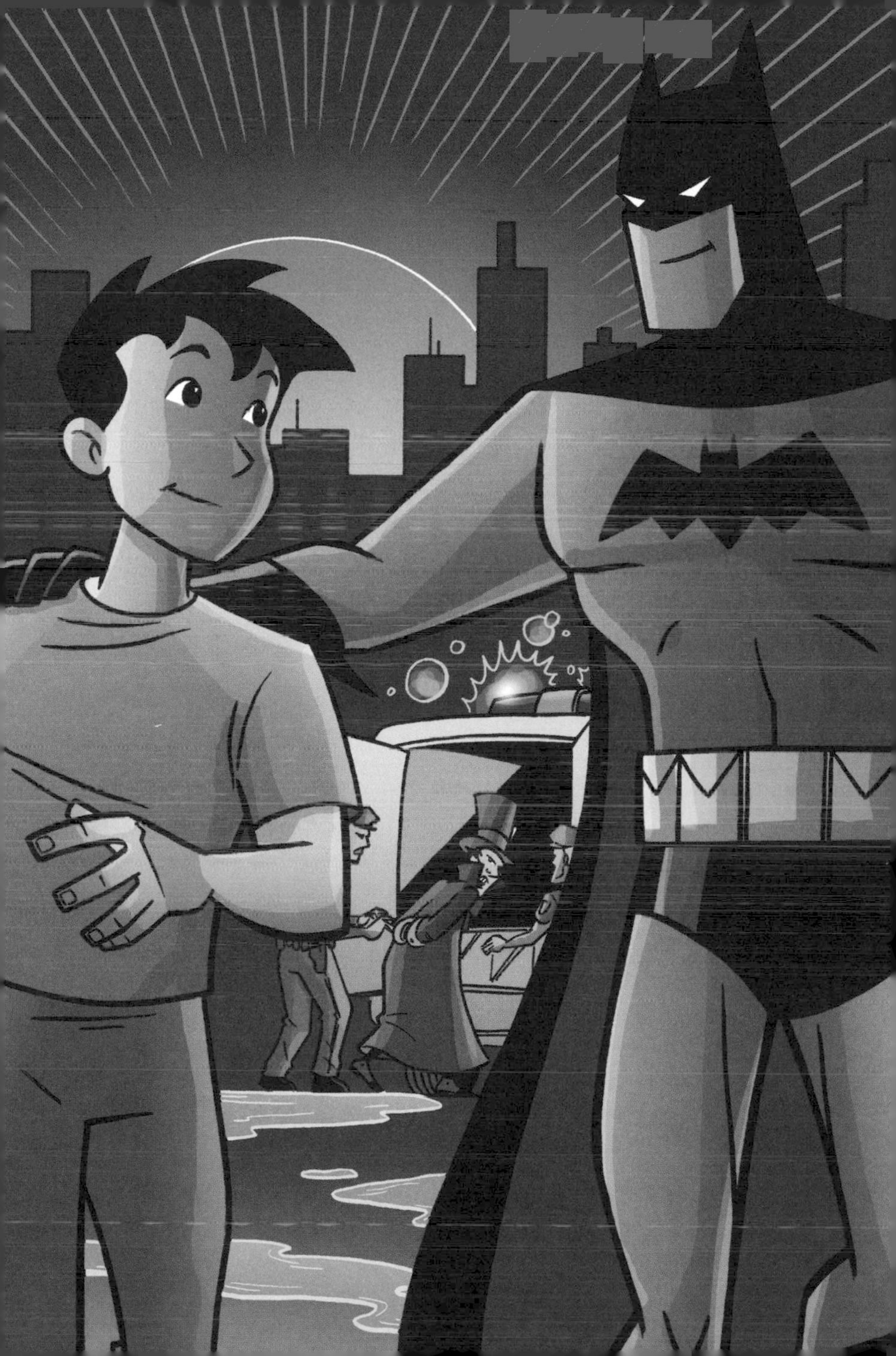

Mad Hatter

REAL NAME: Jervis Tetch

OCCUPATION: Professional Criminal

BASE: Gotham City

HEIGHT:
4 feet 8 inches

WEIGHT:
149 pounds

EYES:
Black

HAIR:
Black

Jervis Tetch is obsessed with Lewis Carroll's book, *Alice's Adventures in Wonderland*. He believes himself to be the Mad Hatter, a crazy hatmaker from Carroll's book, and has taken the name as his own. Tetch is also convinced that Alice, a former coworker, is the main character from *Wonderland*, and that she is destined to marry him. This belief has led Tetch to create mind control technology in order to brainwash Alice, as well as the rest of the world, into living out his crazy fantasy.

G.C.P.D. GOTHAM CITY POLICE DEPARTMENT

- True to his super-villain name, the Mad Hatter is obsessed with hats of all shapes and sizes. His crimes are often hat-themed or involve stealing expensive headwear.

- Tetch is obsessed with the book Alice's Adventures in Wonderland, *as well as its sequel,* Through the Looking Glass. Tetch loves these stories so much that he cannot tell the difference between Wonderland and the real world.

- The Mad Hatter has created several inventions that place other people's minds under his control. He often plants them in hats of varying kinds to catch his victims unprepared. He has also concealed them inside electronic devices, like radios and cell phones, to spread his mind control powers across entire cities.

- Tetch's mind control technology can make his victims stronger, faster, and tougher, thereby turning them into fearsome servants.

CONFIDENTIAL

BIOGRAPHIES

Donald Lemke works as a children's book editor and writer. He is the author of the Zinc Alloy graphic novel adventure series. He also wrote *Captured Off Guard*, a World War II story, and a graphic novelization of *Gulliver's Travels*, both of which were selected by the Junior Library Guild. Most recently, he has written several Batman adventures for DC Super Heroes chapter books.

Gregg Schigiel is originally from South Florida. He knew he wanted to be a cartoonist since he was 11 years old. He's worked on projects featuring Batman, Spider-Man, SpongeBob SquarePants, and just about everything in between. Gregg currently lives and works in New York City.

Lee Loughridge has been working in comics for more than fifteen years. He currently lives in sunny California in a tent on the beach.

GLOSSARY

amused (uh-MYOOZD)—kept someone entertained

brainwash (BRAYN-wahsh)—to make someone accept and believe something

ignition (ig-NISH-uhn)—the electrical system of a vehicle that uses power from the battery to start the engine

marquee (mar-KEE)—a large structure over a theater entrance that displays the name of the movie that's showing

microchip (MYE-kroh-chip)—a very thin device with electronic circuits printed on it. Microchips are used in computers and other electronic equipment.

obedient (oh-BEE-dee-uhnt)—if you are obedient, you do what you are told to do

oversized (OH-vur-sized)—unusually big, or unnecessarily large

paparazzi (pah-puh-RAHT-zee)—photographers of celebrities

usher (UHSH-ur)—someone who shows people to their seats in a church, theater, or stadium

DISCUSSION QUESTIONS

1. Which half of the Dynamic Duo did more to take down the Mad Hatter — Robin or Batman? Why?

2. This book has ten illustrations. Which one is your favorite?

3. Tim Drake's secret identity is Robin. Should a super hero keep his or her true identity a secret? Why or why not?

WRITING PROMPTS

1. Imagine that you're the new Robin. As the Boy Wonder, what skills would you bring to the team as the Dark Knight's partner? Write about it.

2. Robin goes undercover to stop the Mad Hatter. Imagine that you're an undercover detective. What kinds of crimes would you solve?

3. The Mad Hatter invents devices that help him commit crimes. Create your own invention. What is its name? What does it do? Write about your device. Then, draw a picture of it.

WAIT!!
DON'T CLOSE THE BOOK!
THERE'S MORE!
FIND MORE:
GAMES & PUZZLES
HEROES & VILLAINS
AUTHORS & ILLUSTRATORS
AT...
WWW.CAPSTONEKIDS.COM
STILL WANT MORE?
FIND COOL WEBSITES AND MORE BOOKS LIKE THIS ONE AT
WWW.FACTHOUND.COM. JUST TYPE IN THE BOOK ID:
9781434221315 AND YOU'RE READY TO GO!

MORE NEW BATMAN ADVENTURES!

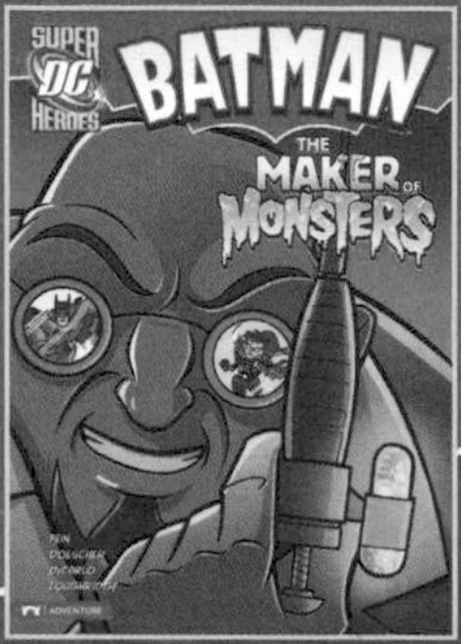
SUPER DC HEROES
BATMAN
THE MAKER OF MONSTERS

THE MAKER OF MONSTERS

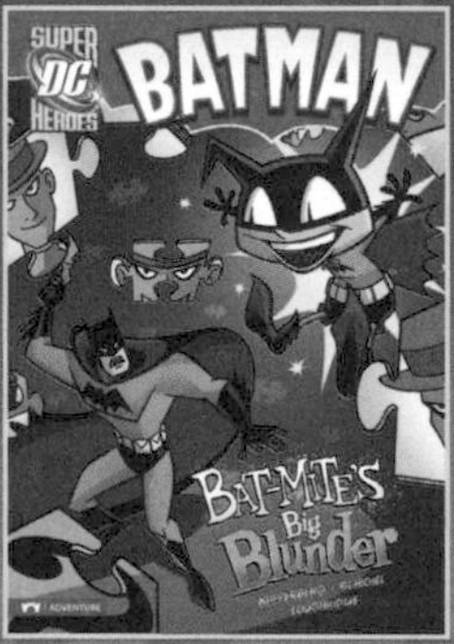
SUPER DC HEROES
BATMAN
BAT-MITE'S Big Blunder

BAT-MITE'S BIG BLUNDER

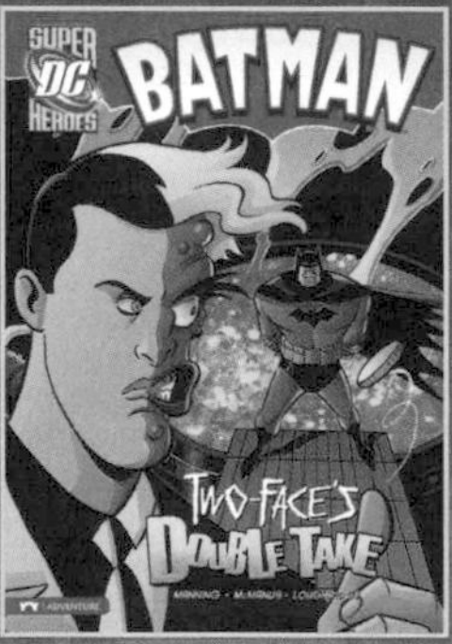
SUPER DC HEROES
BATMAN
TWO-FACE'S DOUBLE TAKE

TWO-FACE'S DOUBLE TAKE

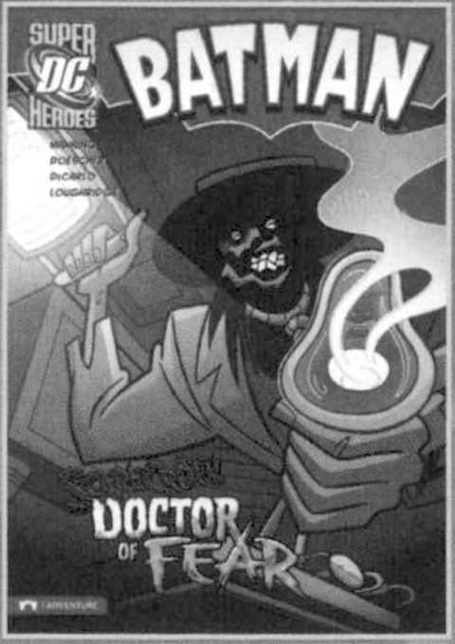
SUPER DC HEROES
BATMAN
DOCTOR OF FEAR

SCARECROW, DOCTOR OF FEAR

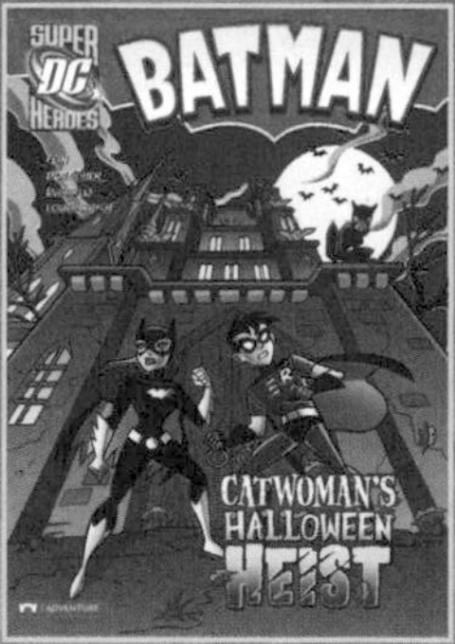
SUPER DC HEROES
BATMAN
CATWOMAN'S HALLOWEEN HEIST

CATWOMAN'S HALLOWEEN HEIST

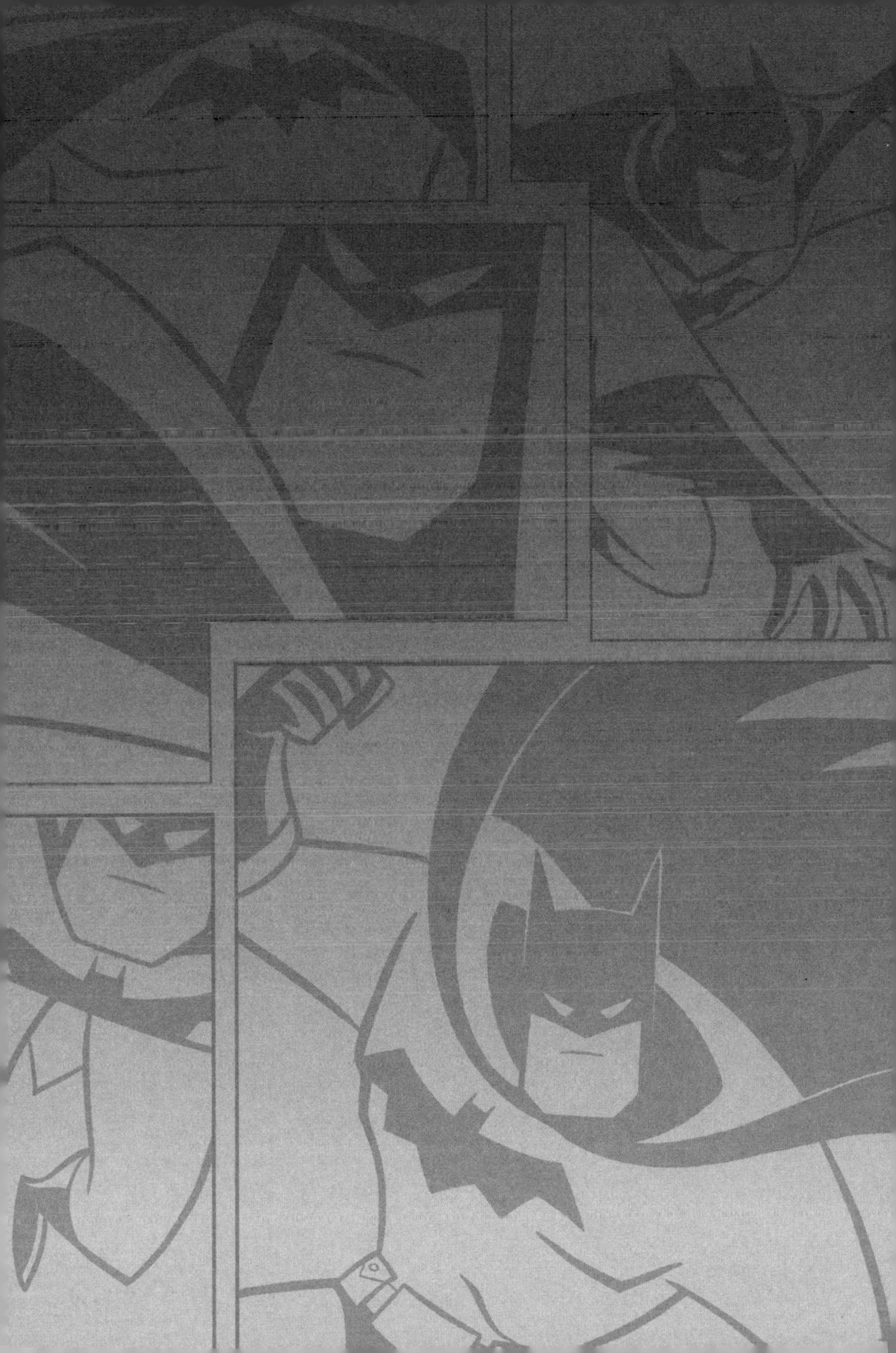

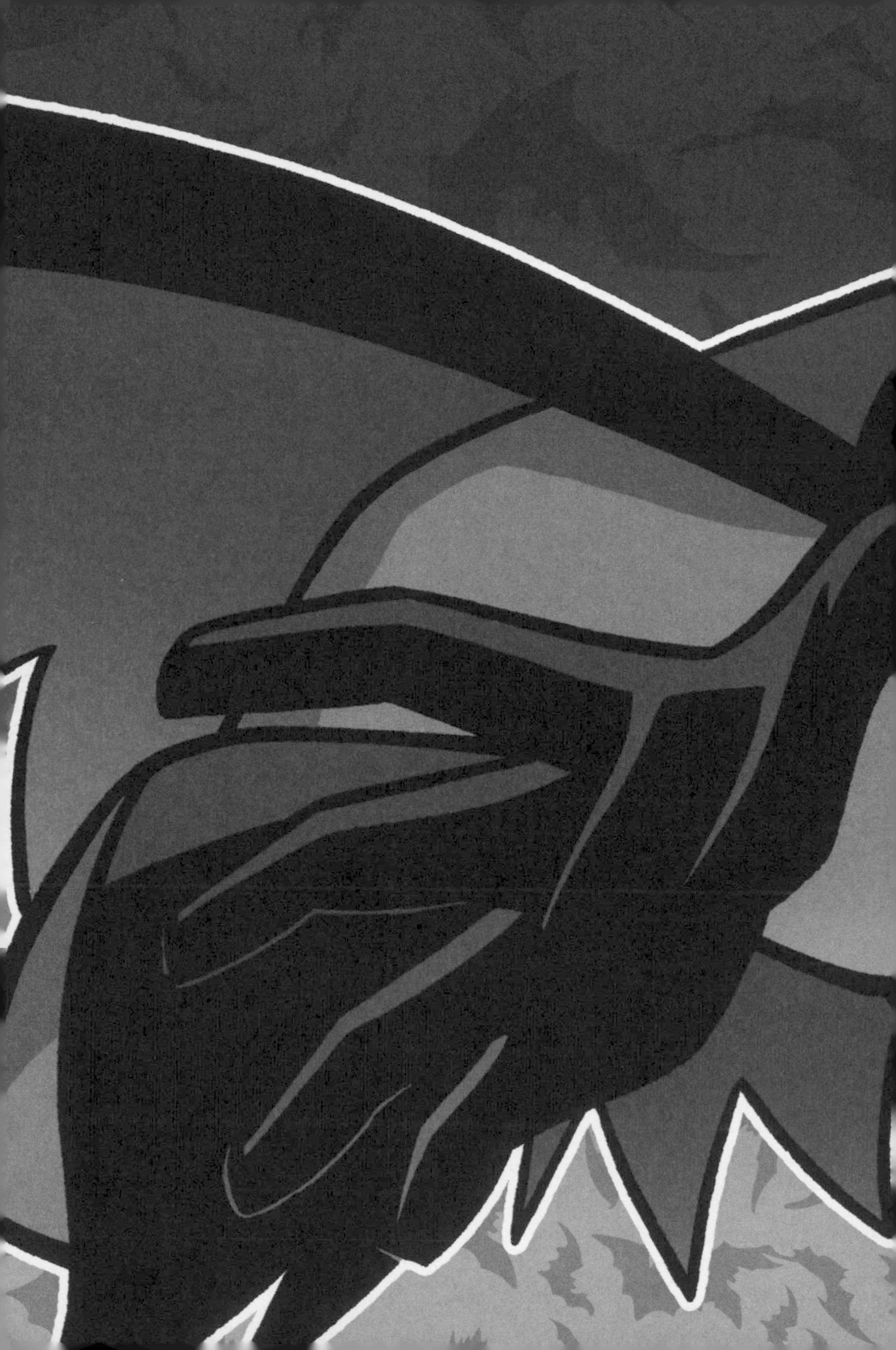

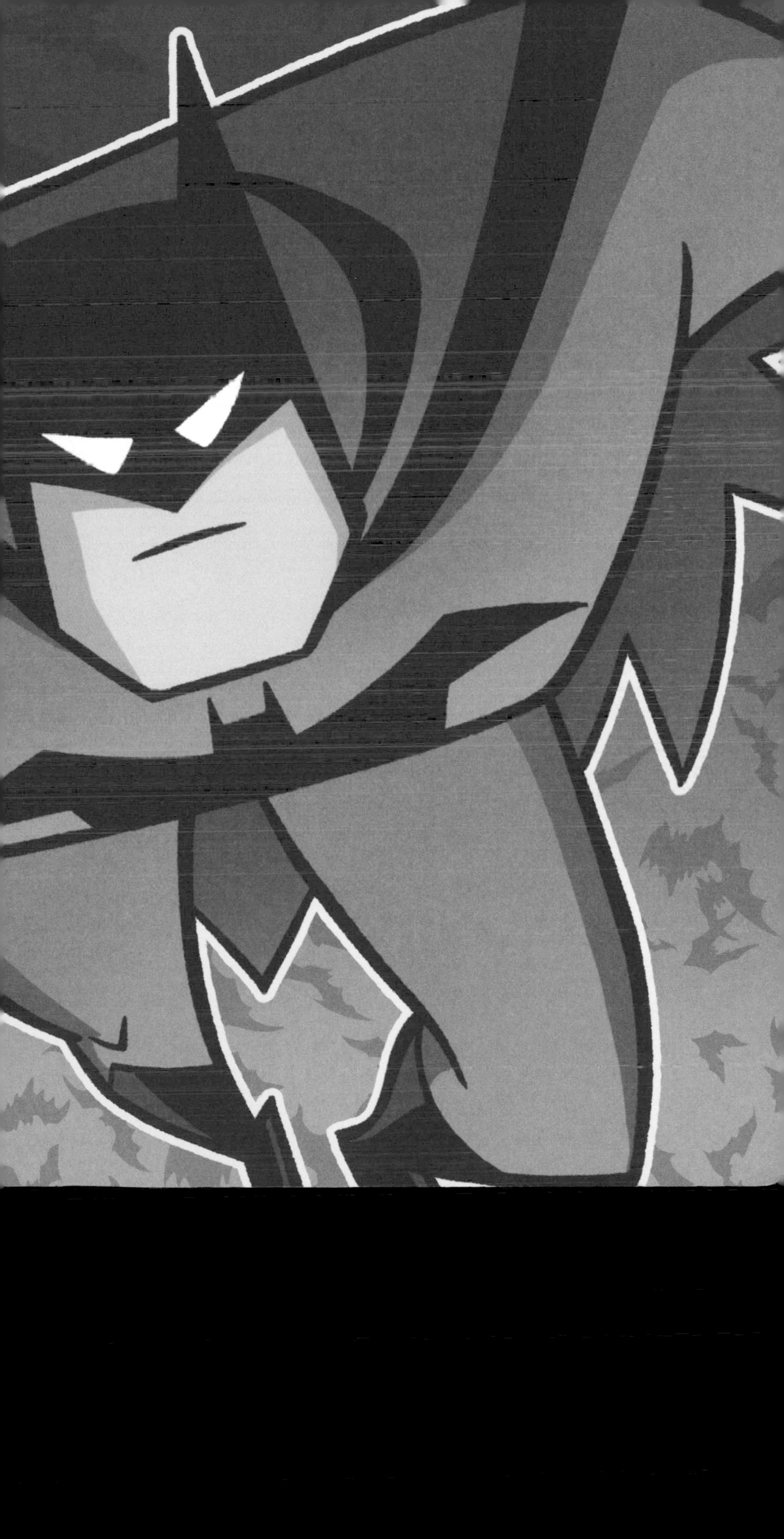